515 ... Wethersfield, CT 06109-2216

HONK!

"Certainly," the witch assured them, the very picture of sympathetic concern. "If I see any sign of your poor missing little boy around here, I'll be sure to send word to you."

Howard stamped his webbed feet.

His mother looked frightened as she hurriedly told the old witch, "Thank you. You're very kind." Then she tugged on Father's sleeve, obviously anxious to get out of there. Her fear for Howard combined with her fear *of* Howard, and tears overflowed her eyes and ran down her cheeks.

"I . . . am . . . Howard," Howard honked so slowly and distinctly they *had* to understand him.

Except they didn't.

Three Good Deeds

OTHER BOOKS BY VIVIAN VANDE VELDE

All Hallows' Eve: 13 Stories
Now You See It . . .
Wizard at Work
Heir Apparent
Being Dead
Alison, Who Went Away
Magic Can Be Murder
The Rumpelstiltskin Problem
There's a Dead Person Following My Sister Around
Never Trust a Dead Man
A Coming Evil
Ghost of a Hanged Man
Smart Dog
Curses, Inc. and Other Stories
Tales from the Brothers Grimm and the Sisters Weird
Companions of the Night
Dragon's Bait
User Unfriendly
A Well-Timed Enchantment
A Hidden Magic

VIVIAN VANDE VELDE

Three
Good Deeds

MAGIC CARPET BOOKS
HARCOURT, INC.
Orlando   Austin   New York   San Diego   London

Copyright © 2005 by Vande Velde, Vivian

All rights reserved. No part of this publication may be reproduced
or transmitted in any form or by any means, electronic or mechanical,
including photocopy, recording, or any information storage and retrieval
system, without permission in writing from the publisher.

Requests for permission to make copies of any part of the work
should be submitted online at www.harcourt.com/contact or mailed
to the following address: Permissions Department, Harcourt, Inc.,
6277 Sea Harbor Drive, Orlando, Florida 32887-6777.

www.HarcourtBooks.com

First Magic Carpet Books edition 2007

Magic Carpet Books is a trademark of Harcourt, Inc.,
registered in the United States of America and/or other jurisdictions.

The Library of Congress has cataloged the hardcover edition as follows:
Vande Velde, Vivian.
Three good deeds/Vivian Vande Velde.
p. cm.
Summary: Caught stealing some goose eggs from a witch, Howard is
cursed for his heartlessness and turned into a goose himself, and he
can only become human again by performing three good deeds.
[1. Geese—Fiction. 2. Witches—Fiction. 3. Behavior—Fiction.
4. Blessing and cursing—Fiction.] I. Title.
PZ7.V2773Thr 2005
[Fic]—dc22 2004029578
ISBN 978-0-15-205382-6
ISBN 978-0-15-205455-7 pb

Text set in Bembo
Designed by Cathy Riggs

A C E G H F D B

Printed in the United States of America

To Nancy and Don,
who are fans of geese but—
as far as I know—
have never *been* geese

Contents

Three Good Deeds

I

Howard

Though all the children of the village of Dumphrey's Mill called the woman whose little house sat at the edge of Goose Pond "the old witch," Howard never suspected till too late that she truly *was* a witch.

She was old and she was ugly, and to the children that was reason enough to call her a witch.

It was also reason enough to tag along behind her those times when she came

into the village to sell milk from her goats
or to buy grain from the miller. Howard
was not the best nor the worst of the children to ever be born in Dumphrey's Mill.
So when the old witch would come to
town, Howard did not suggest it might be
fun to tease her; but neither did he suggest
it might not be nice. Instead, he would
join in with the others and imitate the way
she walked—her shoulders hunched, her
right foot dragging behind her—until
she'd notice and shake her cane at them,
which caused them to flee with delighted
screeches of terror.

One spring day when the witch had *not*
come to town, Howard and his best friend,
Roscoe, noticed the freshly laundered sheets
Roscoe's mother had hung on the line to
dry. Because there was nothing to do, and
because they were boys, they thought the
sheets on the line made a fine cave. One

thing led to another, and in short order the cave was in pretty serious need of more laundering.

At the exact moment Roscoe's mother discovered this, it was Roscoe's turn to be the dragon in the cave; Howard, as the knight, was in the side yard looking for a stick that could pass for a sword. So Roscoe's mother never saw Howard as she dragged Roscoe by the ear into the house, to the accompaniment of some very undragonlike yelps.

Howard *could* have knocked on the door and volunteered the information that the knight versus cave-dragon game had in fact been his idea, but it was too late to save Roscoe anyway, so Howard decided it was no use sacrificing himself for nothing.

But without Roscoe, there was very little excitement in the village of Dumphrey's Mill.

That was when Howard decided he would go to Goose Pond and see if the geese had laid any eggs yet.

Even though the geese there were wild, everyone knew the old witch was very protective of them: As soon as the snow melted every spring, she pulled weeds from the edge of the pond so that when the geese returned from their winter home in the south they would find the area ready for building their nests. And throughout the spring and summer, she threw out crusts of bread for them to eat. When it was time for them to return to the warmth of the south, she would stand on the edge of the pond and shout good-byes, calling each by name.

Howard thought this was ridiculous behavior because everyone knows both geese and goose eggs are for eating.

When Howard arrived at Goose Pond that spring day, he stood hidden at the edge of the trees and looked over the old witch's yard to make sure she wasn't someplace she'd be able to see him.

As there was no sign of her, Howard crept to the edge of the pond and began searching for nests.

He found one quickly.

By the way the goose who'd been sitting there hissed and flapped her wings, Howard could tell that she was indeed guarding eggs.

He waved his cap and managed to startle her away long enough to snatch three of the eight eggs from the nest.

"You don't need so many," he assured her as she tried to peck him.

He set one of the eggs on the edge of the grass and rolled it toward the water's edge to distract the mother goose. This did indeed confuse her. As she rushed to save that one, Howard grabbed another, put all three into his cap, and started to run away.

Except something caught in his feet, and he fell hard.

When he looked up, he saw that what had tripped him had been the old witch's cane.

2

The Old Witch

"You wicked, wicked boy!" the old witch scolded him.

Howard had many fine qualities, but being quick-witted was not chief among them. "What?" he asked to give himself time to think and to give the old witch time in which he hoped she would calm down. "Who, me? Why?" And, when none of those seemed to have any effect, he went back to "What?"

"Coming here to steal my geese's eggs,"

she said. "And it would be bad enough if you wanted to eat them, but to take them just to destroy them is simply wicked."

Howard looked where she was looking. The cap was still in his hand, and the eggs were still in the cap. But the eggs were no longer in their shells. When he'd fallen, the eggs had taken the brunt of his weight. Eggshell shards and sticky egg innards oozed between his fingers.

"Well," Howard pointed out, "it's your own fault. If you hadn't tripped me, I wouldn't have fallen on them."

Howard thought this was sensible reasoning, but the witch did not.

She narrowed her eyes at him and said, "You, young man, are in serious need of a good lesson."

Since this was very similar to what he had just recently overheard Roscoe's mother say as she was twisting Roscoe's ear to get him inside the house, Howard clapped his hands protectively over his own ears—sticky egg mess notwithstanding.

He saw the old witch's lips move as she said something he could not hear and then he felt something unlike anything he'd ever felt before.

It was as though a huge wind was suddenly intent on blowing Howard off his feet. And all the while the wind shoved at him, something was striking him—something softer than hail, but harder than snow. *What* it was, Howard couldn't tell because there was nothing in the air he could see. The sensation didn't hurt, but it was certainly unpleasant.

Like feathers, Howard thought. It was like lots and lots—and lots—of feathers landing on him.

Except that he couldn't see any feathers.

And neither could he see anything—

besides himself—being affected by the wind that was trying so hard to topple him: The trees were still; the grass did not ripple; the clothes of the old witch standing before him were not flapping.

Strange, Howard thought. And while thinking that, he lost his concentration, and the wind succeeded in knocking him to his bottom.

"Ooof!" he puffed—and even in that first moment some part of him recognized his voice had come out louder than he'd expected, and more sharp and nasal.

It also seemed, even though he was sitting down, that the old witch was much too tall looming over him. Or rather, *he* was much too short.

"Hey!" Howard tried to say. In his mind, he could hear the word perfectly clearly.

But to his ears, it definitely came out as *"Honk!"*

3

Goose

Uh-oh, Howard thought. *I guess she really IS a witch.*

He felt *someone* in the village should have warned him that the name referred to more than her age and her looks.

He didn't say this. He said: "What did you do to me?"

It came out: *"Honk honk-honk honk-honk!"*

He stood, and in his standing was not much taller than when he'd been sitting on his bottom. His legs were short and pink and scrawny and ended in huge webbed feet. The tallest thing about him was his long skinny neck. Howard had to concentrate to keep his neck straight so that his head didn't droop. His arms flapped in helpless outrage, arms that were jointed oddly so that they felt more at rest pointing backward than hanging straight down, arms that were covered with grayish brown feathers, arms that were—in fact—wings.

"Honk honk-honk honk-honk!" Howard repeated, more frantic this time.

He was having trouble seeing straight ahead—as though his eyes were too much off to the sides. And what was the huge orange thing that seemed to be following his face around? It moved alarmingly when he asked the old witch what she'd done to him, and to his horror he realized it was attached to his face. It was a goose's beak.

"HONK!" he cried. In his mind he was saying, "Help!" but his beak wouldn't bend to the shape necessary to make the right sound.

Fortunately, the old witch understood goose.

"There is no one to help you," she told Howard.

Though his goose mouth could no longer speak human words, his goose ears could still understand her human speech.

In his agitation, he began flapping his arms, and as he did so, his feet lifted off the ground. Fortunately for Howard, he didn't get too high. He was only up to about eye level with the old witch when he realized he was flying. The reason this was fortunate was because, as soon as he *did* realize, he panicked entirely and froze. This meant Howard stopped flying, abruptly, and landed—*very* abruptly. He tipped over, once again onto his bottom. He noticed there was a lot more to his bottom than there had ever been before.

"There is no one to help you," the old witch repeated—not exactly gloating, but more like explaining. "Except yourself."

Howard fought an inclination to run around in circles flapping his wings and squawking. Looking and talking like a goose was bad enough: He was determined he would not act like one.

He tried to pretend his beak was a set of lips. He tried to speak slowly and distinctly. "What do you mean?" he tried to say.

It came out, *"Honk honk HONK."*

Nobody else, he realized, would be able to understand him. Only the old witch.

She did not answer his question, but instead, she said, "You're a bad boy."

"I'm not a boy at all," Howard honked. "I'm a goose—and that's your fault."

The old witch didn't tell him he had a good point. What she told him was "Well, you'll probably be a bad goose, too."

Howard began to feel sorry for himself. His beady little goose eyes got hot with tears. "My mother doesn't think I'm bad," he protested.

"Mothers never do," the old witch said. "But you come here with your friends—who are *all* bad boys, except for the ones who are bad girls—and you toss pebbles at the geese, and you chase them, and you steal their eggs. Why, just last week, you came here and threw a bucketful of red dye at them. Does your mother know about *that*?"

"That wasn't me," Howard explained. "That was Roscoe." Then, because Roscoe was, after all, his best friend, he added, "It was his sister Gertrude's idea."

What he didn't add was that he had

known all about it. Gertrude had suggested the plan after she had seen Howard's mother mix up the dye to color the wool the family had gathered from their sheep. But it was Howard who poured some of the dye into a bucket and slipped it to Roscoe while his mother's back was turned.

The plan *had been* for Roscoe to wait for Howard to be done helping his mother.

The plan *had been* for the two boys to join Gertrude after she finished her chores, and for the three of them to go to Goose Pond together.

But Roscoe, who could be highly excitable, couldn't wait, and he went by himself.

So it was only fair for Howard to give the old witch Roscoe's name.

But he could see that the old witch wasn't interested in such little details. She didn't care that she had the wrong boy. She understood Howard's honking, but she didn't understand that he shouldn't be punished. She said, "How would you like someone to throw a bucket of red-dyed water onto your head? How would you like someone to steal *your* eggs?"

Howard—who sometimes didn't know when to quit—asked, "Since when do boy geese have eggs?"

"You think you're so smart," the old witch observed. "You have an answer for everything."

"Well, maybe not every—" Howard started.

The old witch spoke right over him. "You won't be able to talk your way out of this."

"But *you said,*" Howard honked at her. "You said nobody could help me except myself. That means something *can* be done. Besides, you can't keep me a goose forever. My father will come looking for me."

"Will your father know to come here?" the old witch asked.

That was a good point, though a bad outlook—for Howard had not told anyone where he was going.

Not only could the old witch understand goose language, she was also good at reading the expression on his little goose face. Perhaps it was that the lower portion of his beak began to quiver. "It won't be forever," she told him. "Just until you've learned your lesson—until you're no longer a bad boy."

"Oh, I've learned my lesson," Howard assured her. "I'll be a much better boy from now on. I am very, very, very, very sorry for what I did."

Howard waited to return to human shape.

And waited.

And waited.

"Why am I not changing back?" he asked.

"Because you haven't proven yourself."

"Well?" Howard honked at the old witch impatiently. "How do I do that?"

"By doing three good deeds," she told him. "Good luck to you." She started walking back to her cottage with her back bent and her foot dragging.

Three good deeds.

Three didn't sound so bad. Three was better than, for example, one hundred.

So long as they weren't three hard deeds.

He shouted after her, "Which three?"

She didn't even stop walking. "Any three."

Howard thought about this. He thought about his arms that were wings. He thought about his short little legs. He thought about his voice that came out as honks. "How can I do three good deeds if I'm a goose?"

The witch had reached her cottage. She opened the door. She called over her shoulder, "Try hard." Then she shut the door behind her.

Try hard? What kind of advice was "Try hard"?

"That's stupid!" Howard shouted at the closed door. "And mean." Then, even though it was fairly strong proof that he wasn't nearly as sorry as he knew he needed to be, he added, "And you're old and ugly, too."

The sound of his honking faded, and Howard was alone in the stillness of the day.

4

Plans

Howard considered what he might do. *I could just walk up to that door,* he thought. *I could kick it in, and I could shake that old witch and MAKE her change me back into a boy.*

He looked at his floppy webbed feet— though he had to turn his head sideways because his eyes were too far back on his face for him to look straight ahead. He looked at his wings, which still seemed like bent-the-wrong-way arms rather than any

useful body part. He realized there probably wouldn't be much kicking-in or
shaking-sense-into going on for a while.

"Mother?" he tried his voice out.
"Father?"

It was no use practicing anything more
complicated. His words came out a qua-
very honk. How could he explain to his
parents that something bad had happened
when geese were limited to honking,
quacking, and the occasional hissing?

Howard waddled to the edge of the
pond and looked at his reflection. Never
mind that he looked silly. He tipped his
head this way and that, hoping to catch a
glimpse of something a loving parent could
recognize despite the feathers.

"Help," he moaned. But he knew there
was no one to help. He went from sad to
frightened, and his honking for help got
louder.

Nobody would ever know what had happened to him. He went from frightened to angry, and his honking got louder yet.

Howard's ears were ringing from all the noise he was making. He went from angry to having a plan, and he honked as loudly as he could. The old witch did not seem to be the kind of person who had a lot of patience. Surely he could eventually annoy her into changing her mind.

"Help! Help! Help! Help! Help!" he honked as loudly as his little goose lungs would allow. His little goose lungs did a fine job. His honking hurt his ears and his throat. His honking echoed under the sky.

But his noise did not make the old witch change her mind.

Howard's honking slowed down from frantic to tired to defeated. He let his too-long neck sag. His feathers drooped. The old witch had more stamina than he did. He stopped honking altogether.

There was a rustling in the weeds at the edge of the pond.

Howard jumped backward. His wings beat at the air, but he was in enough trouble as it was without trying to fly. After all, his goose body might know how but his boy brain knew flying was not one of his natural talents. What if he froze again, and this time fell from a great height?

Or what if he could fly too well, and he went so far that he got lost, and then even if he *did* do the old witch's stupid three good deeds, he couldn't find his way back to tell her about it so she could return him to his real form?

Or what if the old witch realized she'd been much too harsh with him and that it really was Roscoe she should have punished, and she changed her mind but she couldn't find him—or worse yet, turned him back into a boy while he was up in the air?

So, no flying.

"Who's there?" he demanded in his fiercest goose hiss.

"Sorry," a voice honked at him, soft and uncertain as a honk could be. "I didn't mean to startle you. I was just wondering what was wrong."

Recent experience had turned Howard into a suspicious goose. "You didn't answer my question," he pointed out. "Who are you?"

The tall weeds parted just the tiniest bit. Howard caught a glimpse of a goose's beak. "Well, so far I have been called Moonlight-Gives-Her-Down-a-Silver-Glow."

Howard snorted. "That has to be the silliest name I've ever heard."

There was a sniffle from the other goose. "I'm sorry," she said, as though her name were her fault. She still didn't step out from her hiding place. "What's your name?"

"Howard."

"How-Word," the other goose repeated carefully as though she'd never heard that name before. Then she said, "I've been called Moonlight-Gives-Her-Down-a-Silver-Glow since the time I was little more than a hatchling and I got separated from my brothers and sisters. Our parents searched for the rest of the day, but they couldn't find me until after the moon rose and shed its light on the pond. How did you come to be called How-Word?"

"Oh," Howard said. He had no idea how his parents had chosen his name. Rather than admit that, he asked, "Why do you keep talking like your name's about to change?"

Still hidden, for the most part, behind the weeds, Moonlight-Gives-Her-Down-a-Silver-Glow gave a shuddery sigh. "Well," she said, "you know how geese can be."

"I do?" Howard asked. He knew how people could be, and wondered if that was the same.

"I'm afraid once they see what's happened to me, they'll call me cruel names, and one of those will stick, and then I'll be called that for the rest of my life."

So apparently geese and people *did* have something in common.

"What's happened to you?" Howard asked.

Moonlight-Gives-Her-Down-a-Silver-Glow must have taken a step back, because even her beak disappeared among the fronds of the water weeds. "Oh," she said, sounding distressed, "never mind. I'll just go now."

She sounded as miserable as Howard felt. And she was the one person . . . well, the one creature . . . who had shown any concern while he'd been calling for help.

Howard stumbled upon just the right thing to say. He said, "*I* would never call you a cruel name no matter what it is that's happened to you." He said this even though just the past summer he had called Roscoe's sister Gertrude "Baldy" when her mother had to cut her hair really short because of an infestation of lice.

"You wouldn't?" Moonlight-Gives-Her-Down-a-Silver-Glow asked. "That's very kind of you."

It felt nice to be called kind. Curious, Howard again asked, "What *did* happen to you?"

"Are you sure you won't laugh?"

"No matter what," Howard assured her.

The blades of grass separated. Moonlight-Gives-Her-Down-a-Silver-Glow moved very, very slowly. At first Howard couldn't see anything wrong: She had only one head; she had two big dark eyes, a beak that seemed to be the right shape and size, two feet, a pair of wings. . . .

"It's all right," he encouraged her, because she was lingering in the shadow of the weeds and he couldn't get a good look. Something—he was assuming some nearby plant—seemed to be casting a red sheen to the feathers on her head and back so that he couldn't see what was the problem. "You look fine to me," he said. He wondered if—like himself—she wasn't supposed to be a goose. On the other hand, he guessed, with her strange name, she probably wasn't supposed to be a human, either. "Did the old witch put a spell on you?" he asked.

"No," said Moonlight-Gives-Her-Down-a-Silver-Glow. "It was a human boy."

And that was when Howard realized that the red sheen wasn't from something reflecting on her. Moonlight-Gives-Her-Down-a-Silver-Glow wore exactly the same red color as his mother's newly dyed woolens.

5

Red

"Oh," Howard said.

Moonlight-Gives-Her-Down-a-Silver-Glow's head drooped. Her body slouched. Her tail feathers sagged. She shuffled backward into the weeds again. "Sorry," she mumbled as though her appearance was an offense. "You won't call me names after all, will you?" she asked in a honk that trembled. "I know I look ridiculous. You won't tell the others?"

"I said I wouldn't," Howard reminded

her. Then he realized what she'd said about the others. He asked, "Have you been hiding since this happened?"

"I was hoping it would go away"—Moonlight-Gives-Her-Down-a-Silver-Glow sighed—"before anybody saw me."

"Of course it will go away," Howard assured her, knowing that dyes fade. Eventually. Usually.

He saw her perk up and thought that surely, for a goose who spent so much time in the water, the dye would fade sooner rather than later.

Except, of course, that she wasn't going into the water for fear of being seen and laughed at. She could spend the whole summer long hiding in the weeds.

"But . . . ," he said, and he saw the hope fade from her eyes. So he changed to: "But meanwhile you look fine. You look different in a good way. You look exotic and . . ."

What he wanted to say was that she looked—between gray-brown feathers and red dye—like a moth-eaten tea cozy. Instead he finished, "You look interesting."

Moonlight-Gives-Her-Down-a-Silver-Glow poked her head back out from among the weeds. "'Interesting?'" she repeated. "Is that good?"

It would be easy to make her feel bad, but it was just as easy to make her feel good.

"Absolutely," Howard said.

Someone—some goose—was paddling around in the pond and noticed Howard. "Hey!" this other goose said. "You're new. You need to come introduce yourself."

Howard turned to this other goose. "I'm not staying long," he explained. He very much hoped he wouldn't be staying long.

The other goose craned his neck to see

around Howard. "Who's that with you?" he asked. "Moonlight, is that you?"

"This," said Howard, waddling out of the way to let the goose in the pond see Moonlight - Gives - Her - Down - a - Silver - Glow, "is . . ."

Hmmm, what was another way to say *red*?

"This is Sunset."

Sunset was obviously way too short a name to replace something like *Moonlight-Gives-Her-Down-a-Silver-Glow.*

Howard cleared his throat. Luckily, when a goose clears its throat, there's a lot of throat to clear and this gave Howard a lot of time to think. He started again. "This is Sunset Shining . . . Excuse me. Ahem . . . Sunset *Dances* . . . um . . . Like Flames . . ."—inspired, he finished all in a rush—"on Her Feathers. Sunset-Dances-

Like-Flames-on-Her-Feathers. Isn't she
beautiful?"

"Ooh, I like that," whispered the goose
formerly known as Moonlight-Gives-Her-
Down-a-Silver-Glow. "Thank you."

Perhaps it was that not many people
had had occasion to say "Thank you" to
Howard. He felt a bubbling sensation—
not exactly good, not exactly bad, but definitely strange—that started inside, then in
the space of four or five heartbeats grew
and burst through his skin with such force
that he looked down at himself to see if his
feathers were rippling.

From behind him came a voice, a
human voice. "See? That wasn't so hard,
was it?"

The old witch was standing with a basket over her arm. She reached in and tossed
a handful of bread crumbs into the pond.

Sunset-Dances-Like-Flames-on-Her-Feathers dove into the water, and she and the other goose began gobbling up the soggy bread.

"What wasn't so hard?" Howard demanded.

"Doing a good deed," the old witch said.

"Complimenting a goose is a good deed?" Howard asked.

"Making her feel better is."

Howard considered that notion while the witch reached into her basket and threw out more crumbs. So the bubbly feeling was the boy-into-goose spell starting to come apart. He wondered if he would look one-third boy and two-thirds goose, because that would be very weird—though it might make doing the remaining two good deeds easier.

But, no. He still looked entirely goose.

Other geese had heard the happy honking and splashing of Sunset-Dances-Like-Flames-on-Her-Feathers and the other goose and were beginning to swim their way.

Howard took a deep breath. Then another. Then he said to the old witch, "Have I mentioned what lovely eyes you have?"

He waited for the bubbly feeling to indicate the spell loosening up further.

Nothing.

"Nice try," the old witch said, with a very unlovely snort. "A certain amount of sincerity might help. Want some bread?" She tossed a crust at his webbed feet.

Howard prodded the bread with his toe and found it as hard as the stone it had landed by. "This stale old thing?" he scoffed. His mother would never let bread go that stale. She'd toss it out to the animals rather than feed it to her family.

Oh, Howard thought, realizing the old witch was doing just that.

She suggested, "Dunk it in the water."

The water was muddy and had geese swimming in it.

Howard heard Sunset-Dances-Like-Flames-on-Her-Feathers getting introduced as more and more geese gathered. Howard heard the geese-honks for "one of a kind" and "beautiful" and "interesting." Geese did not strike him as being very original thinkers.

"Your bread probably has weevils in it," Howard said to the old witch. She wanted a sincere compliment? He didn't need to compliment her at all when there was a whole pond full of gullible geese nearby. "Besides, I'm not going to be a goose long enough to get hungry."

The old witch shrugged, and Howard eased himself into the pond. He planned to wade in only as far as his short legs would permit since he didn't know how to swim; but as soon as his goose body hit the water, his goose instincts took over. His feet began paddling and in moments he was gliding away from the shore.

He swam up to Sunset-Dances-Like-Flames-on-Her-Feathers and said, "Wow! You look even better in the full sun than you did back there in the shadow of the weeds."

"Thank you," she said to him between mouthfuls of watery bread.

Howard watched the water squish out from her beak and waited for the spell-loosening sensation to start.

Nothing happened.

Maybe a compliment only worked once for each . . . complimentee?

Howard swam up to another goose. "You have very soft-looking feathers."

"Thank you," that one said, though she sounded a bit timid, as though distrusting why he'd come up to her to say this.

Still nothing. Maybe the compliment wasn't good enough.

To another goose, Howard said, "The sparkles in the water cast sparkles in your eyes. Very becoming."

"Thanks," said that goose, but she backed away from him warily, as though he made her nervous.

"My, you're such a good swimmer," Howard said to yet another goose. "I bet you could teach all of us a thing or two about swimming."

The goose ignored him.

"Love the shade of orange of your beak," Howard called out to another.

That one lowered its head and hissed, a hiss Howard understood as "Keep your distance, new youngling." Now it was Howard's turn to back up.

He backed into Sunset-Dances-Like-Flames-on-Her-Feathers, who stopped in her bread-gobbling to warn Howard, "That's Mighty-Beak/Bone-Crusher. You probably don't want to get on his bad side."

Mighty-Beak/Bone-Crusher?

Did someone with a name like that *have* a good side?

This wasn't fair. Howard was trying to be sincere.

He returned to the shore, to see if that crust of bread was still there because maybe he was going to be stuck as a goose for a little longer than he'd hoped.

But both witch and bread were gone.

6

Pond Life

Now that the bread was gone, the geese began to disperse.

"Sunset!" Howard called to the only one—human or animal—who had been friendly to him this afternoon.

Sunset-Dances-Like-Flames-on-Her-Feathers was swimming side by side with Mighty-Beak/Bone-Crusher.

Both geese turned to face him. Mighty-Beak/Bone-Crusher hissed at him, so Howard didn't swim any closer.

"What do geese eat," Howard asked, "when there isn't an old witch to throw bread at you?"

Sunset-Dances-Like-Flames-on-Her-Feathers laughed as though she thought Howard was making a joke. "How-Word, you're so funny."

Mighty-Beak/Bone-Crusher honked, "How-Word? I don't like this newcomer, How-Word."

"Well . . . ," Howard said. He debated between *What makes you think I care?* and *I don't like you, either,* but he remembered Sunset-Dances-Like-Flames-on-Her-Feathers saying, "You probably don't want to get on his bad side." Mighty-Beak/Bone-Crusher was significantly bigger than Howard and had a swagger to his swim. And his beak did look impressively sharp and strong.

Mighty-Beak/Bone-Crusher laughed at

Howard's silence, but it wasn't pleasant like the laugh of Sunset-Dances-Like-Flames-on-Her-Feathers. "This How-Word isn't the bravest goose in the pond, is he?"

Howard took a deep breath, decided—yet again—against arguing, then admitted, "No."

Sunset-Dances-Like-Flames-on-Her-Feathers came to his defense. "How-Word is nice," she said. "He talked me out of the weeds when I was being shy."

Apparently Mighty-Beak/Bone-Crusher wasn't interested in Howard's good qualities. "You stay away from my female," he warned. "She is one of a kind and beautiful."

This time Howard couldn't stop himself. He told Sunset-Dances-Like-Flames-on-Her-Feathers, "You could do better. Where was *he* all the while you were afraid to show yourself?"

Mighty-Beak/Bone-Crusher charged at Howard, flapping his wings and honking.

Howard found out that geese could swim backward—quickly.

Sunset-Dances-Like-Flames-on-Her-Feathers turned away from both the males and kept on swimming in the direction she'd been heading before. Howard didn't know if she was abandoning him, or trying to get Mighty-Beak/Bone-Crusher to follow her and leave him alone.

Mighty-Beak/Bone-Crusher called after Howard, "Your feathers are dull; your neck is short; and the webbing between your toes is too thin."

"Oh yeah?" Howard honked from a safe distance. He guessed these were goose insults, and he wanted to get back at Mighty-Beak/Bone-Crusher. What would be a bad thing to have someone say about you if you were a goose? Howard said, "I know ducks who are better looking than you!"

Mighty-Beak/Bone-Crusher came at Howard again, somewhere between swimming and flying, so he looked like he was practically walking on the surface of the water. Whatever the geese called that move, it was *fast*.

Howard scrambled back up onto the shore, wondering if Mighty-Beak/Bone-Crusher would follow him onto land.

Sunset-Dances-Like-Flames-on-Her-Feathers continued to act as though she'd forgotten all about the two of them. She honked a greeting to another goose, and that got Mighty-Beak/Bone-Crusher's attention off Howard. "Stop talking to everybody," he complained to her. "You're with me."

"If I'm with you," she snapped, "then why are you over there chasing How-Word?"

Mighty-Beak/Bone-Crusher hesitated for one more glare at Howard. In a honk very like a snarl, he told Howard, "You're unfit to father eggs."

"I should hope so," Howard muttered after him.

He watched Mighty-Beak/Bone-Crusher catch up to Sunset-Dances-Like-Flames-on-Her-Feathers, who was swimming in circles while she waited for him.

At the last moment, just before facing around the other way, she said, louder than strictly necessary if it was meant only for Mighty-Beak/Bone-Crusher to hear, "Let's find some nice plants to eat."

Howard liked to think she was speaking to him, that she had realized maybe he hadn't been joking when he asked what geese ate.

But which plants? None of the ones around the pond looked appetizing, like apples or berries or even carrots. He looked down at the weed he was standing nearest to and watched a small pale worm crawl across the broad leaf.

It'll probably become obvious, he thought, *once I get hungry enough.*

But he wasn't going to let himself get that hungry.

He was going to go home and—somehow or other—let his parents know what had happened.

Surely they could help him.

He hoped.

7

Dumphrey's Mill

At first, Howard's plan was to walk back home, because the thought of flying was too scary. But his short goose legs made for a slow pace, and his webbed goose feet got tired very quickly.

I'll fly, he thought, *but I just won't fly very high*.

He flapped his wings and got himself up to the height from which he was used to seeing the road.

And flew smack into the trunk of a tree.

He picked himself up, more stunned than hurt, though his beak *was* sore. A squirrel chattered at him from the branch of another tree. The witch's spell hadn't given Howard the ability to understand any other animal besides geese, but he was sure the squirrel was laughing at him.

"That's easy for you to say," he honked after it. "*Your* eyes are in the front of your face where they belong." Howard tipped his head for a better look. "More or less." He shook himself to make sure nothing was broken, and muttered, "Stupid squirrel."

Walking was safer, but at the rate he was traveling, it would take him forever to get through the woods around Goose Pond and back to Dumphrey's Mill.

Once more, Howard began to fly, but it was difficult to get used to seeing things off to the sides better than he could see what was directly in front of him. And he quickly found he was getting dizzy from swiveling his head left and right to avoid trees.

Maybe, he thought, *it would be easier if I flew just a little higher—just above tree level.*

The trouble was, once he got there, the canopy of treetops blocked his view of the path.

He was sure that—without the path to guide him—he'd get all turned around and become lost forever because of his unusual perspective, for certainly the world looked different at tree level than at human boy level. So Howard kept alternating: flying up just high enough to avoid the trees so that his belly practically skimmed the highest branches, then dipping down to make sure he was still following the path.

Then, finally, he could see where the trees thinned and Dumphrey's Mill started.

Howard flew out from among the trees near the mill itself and almost collided with his friend Alina and her father, who were just coming out of the mill.

"Look out!" Alina called to her father, who was adjusting the sack of grain he carried on his shoulder.

Her father ducked, despite the fact that Howard had already swerved to avoid him and landed in a flurry of feathers and street dust.

"Honk!" Howard said. Did it sound a little like *help*? Howard was sure it did. But Alina's father only said, "Wow! Look at that fat goose!"

Fat? Howard thought. Still, he refused to let himself get distracted by personal insults.

"Honk!" he repeated—much more distinctly, he was positive.

"And stupid, too," Alina's father said.

And he'd always been so friendly to Howard before.

"*Honk!*" Howard said, but peevishly thinking, *Who's being stupid?*

"Here," Alina's father said, shifting the bag of milled grain to Alina's shoulder, "you hold this, and I'll grab him." He was speaking in a soft voice as though he thought Howard was a goose who could understand human speech but was hard of hearing. "We'll have him in your mother's cooking pot before he knows what hit him."

Cooking pot?

It took a moment for the words to sink in, and Howard leaped into the air just as Alina's father lunged.

"*HOOONK!*" Howard called down to him, a nasty word in goose or human.

"Maybe he'll land again," Alina told her father. "We haven't had goose in ages."

What kind of friend was she? He'd always laughed at all her jokes and had even once given her a four-leaf clover he'd found. Too bad Roscoe was confined to the house. He *had* to have more sense than these two.

Alina's father swiped his hat in the air, an attempt to net Howard that came no closer than to stir the air near him. Still, Howard flew a little higher. *Who needs you?* he thought. *MY father is smart enough to recognize the difference between a goose for cooking and a goose who is—in fact—a boy.*

Howard began flying toward his house.

Something thumped against his tail.

Howard squawked. Wheeling around, he saw that Alina's father had picked up a handful of stones and even now was flinging a second one at Howard.

"*HOOONK!*" Howard called again, though that stone missed completely.

Howard began flying a little higher, a little faster.

But other people were calling to one another, pointing him out, laughing, talking about parsley and cherry sauce and turnip stuffing, all the while flinging more stones. One hit Howard on his already-sore beak.

Howard could see his house, but he didn't dare land. These people would jump on him and have him plucked and basted before he could even *try* to communicate.

And what if his own parents, not recognizing him, joined in the chase?

That was just too scary a thought.

Howard angled upward and flew high into the sky, until his friends and neighbors who wanted to bake, stew, or fricassee him were far below, looking as small as he felt. He even forgot to worry about getting lost.

"It's not fair!" Howard honked, as though the old witch could hear him.

"Trying to show myself to my mother so she doesn't worry—surely that qualifies as a good deed."

But he felt none of the bubbling sensation to indicate the spell was loosening its hold on him.

"It *isn't* fair," he repeated.

That was the point at which he looked down and thought, *I'm flying. I'm up higher in the sky than any other person has ever been.*

He began to wobble.

Which made him nervous, so that he concentrated on his flying, on what he was doing.

Which, in turn, made him remember that he had no idea what he was doing.

Which made him begin to drop.

Howard saw the faraway ground begin to come closer. *That* didn't help the wobbles one bit. Howard tried to remember if both wings were supposed to flap together or one at a time. He tried to remember what exact position they should be in.

Howard closed his eyes and felt the on-rush of air ruffle his feathers. *I'm a goose,* he reminded himself, then corrected that to *I'm in a goose body.*

The goose body took over. His wings began to flap properly; the air stopped whistling by his beak and instead supported him.

Howard peeked his eyes open.

He wobbled again, but he didn't let himself think about it. *Enjoy,* he tried to convince himself. *Enjoy.*

From this high up, even the treetops were far away. In the midst of all that green, he could see a blue-gray shape that he realized was Goose Pond. The clearing containing Dumphrey's Mill was unmistakable, too, from this height, and he realized he would not have gotten lost—just the opposite: Finding his way home would have been easier from the air than from close to the ground.

But he couldn't go home, he realized. Not in this shape.

He would have to wait for his parents to come to him. Once he didn't return, of course they would get worried. They would start searching, first closer to home, then farther. Their search would *have* to eventually lead to Goose Pond.

How long could it possibly take?

8

Reunion

What it took, for Howard's parents to show up looking for him, was three long days.

In that time Howard not only learned which plants to eat, but he also learned that no matter how much he ate, he was still going to be hungry.

Maybe it was because the male geese always seemed to want to run him off from wherever he was, so he was constantly moving.

"That's my female!" they would honk, even when he wasn't all that close to anybody, even when he wasn't trying to talk to anybody, even when he had his back turned on everybody and somebody had come up behind *him*. "That's my female!"

And they would honk and hiss and flap their wings until Howard moved far enough away to satisfy one goose, which would generally mean he'd crossed over into some other goose's territory.

Of course, the male geese thinking Howard was too close to their females was nothing compared to parent geese thinking he was too close to their goslings that were just starting to hatch. "Keep away from my family!" mother and father geese would screech at him when the tiny goslings were so far away Howard could hardly make them out. "Danger, children!

Danger! Don't let the newcomer, How-Word, steal you away! Bad stranger! Bad!"

"Really," Howard tried to assure the nervous parents, "I'm not interested in stealing any of your children."

But his denials just seemed to convince them he was up to no good.

If he wasn't being chased away from other geese, he was being chased away from his food. "That's my water lily!" a goose would say as soon as Howard found something that looked good to eat.

"There's lots," Howard would point out.

But if geese weren't too good at thinking, apparently they were even worse at sharing.

Family members would look out for one another, but there was no one to look out for Howard. So he would spend his day swimming and nibbling, swimming and nibbling, swimming and nibbling.

And swimming.

And being hungry.

Another problem Howard had was that everything he ate seemed to go right through him. At first he thought there was something wrong with his stomach. Multiple times a day, he would need to go squat behind a bush to poop green poop. As if that weren't bad enough, as soon as the other geese couldn't see Howard, they suspected he had found a tasty treat that he was trying to keep from them, and they would come looking for him, honking, "Where's How-Word?" "Where's How-Word?" "What is that How-Word up to now?"

In any case, he soon realized that his stomach worked as well as everybody else's: Geese just seemed to go a lot. They didn't need to go in a particular place: If they were in the water at the time they had to go, they'd go in the water everybody swam in; if they were on land, they certainly didn't seem to mind if anybody was watching.

Wondering about that, Howard started wondering about other things—such as his clothes. When the old witch had changed him into a goose, there had been no left-over pile of clothing on the bank of the pond, so he knew his clothing had changed with him. His clothes must, he reasoned, be his feathers.

Now he was living in his clothes all the time, swimming in them, sleeping in them, never changing them, never cleaning them. Every once in a while, when flapping his wings or when shaking the water off himself after he came out of the pond, a feather would come loose, and he would think,

There goes a patch of my shirt. Unless new feathers came in, he would lose his clothing bit by bit.

And some of those missing bits would be in embarrassing places.

What if he accomplished the old witch's stupid three good deeds and she changed him back into a boy who had to walk to town with major portions of his clothing gone? What if he turned back into a naked boy?

But that couldn't be, he assured himself. The geese all lost feathers periodically, so they must grow new ones to replace the old, or after a while every goose would look plucked and ready for a cook pot.

So these were the kinds of things that had come to occupy Howard's mind, when he looked up on that third day of being a goose and saw his parents walking up the path to the old witch's cottage.

"Mother!" he honked. "Father!"

Neither of them glanced his way. Instead they knocked on the old witch's door.

Howard beat his wings and took to the air. The other geese honked and fretted at his sudden movement—perhaps thinking he might have spotted some danger, perhaps just objecting to his starting to fly without declaring his intention: Geese, Howard had quickly come to realize, didn't have the mental capacity to enjoy surprises.

Several other geese rose from the water, but they quickly settled back down again, murmuring, "It's just How-Word being How-Word again."

So Howard was alone when he landed on the little patch of grass where his parents were standing talking to the old witch. "Mother, Father!" he honked.

Still they ignored him.

The old witch was saying, "A little boy?" and shaking her head. "No, I've seen no little boy."

"Here!" Howard honked. "Here I am! She has *too* seen me! She changed me into a goose!"

Honking, Howard rushed at his parents, and it turned out his father *did* see him, for he stuck his leg out to keep Howard at a distance. Howard tried to get around him, and Father kicked him. "Ouch!" Howard honked.

Well, forget Father then. "Mother!" Howard honked, trying to get around Father's leg. "It's me! It's Howard!"

But Father put himself between Howard and Mother as though Mother needed to be protected from him.

Still, Mother was looking directly at him. Of course a mother could recognize her child, enchantment or not. She could tell the old witch was lying. The bond of motherhood's love was stronger than magic or time or any other force of nature. Howard stood tall and looked directly into her eyes. *She'll tell Father it's me,* Howard thought, *and Father will MAKE that old witch change me back.*

"What—," Mother demanded, and Howard knew she was going to challenge the witch with *What have you done to my son?* "What," Mother demanded, "is the matter with that goose?"

Goose? GOOSE? Mother thought he was just another goose?

"Is it dangerous?" Mother asked, her voice shivering. "Will it bite?"

Father began swinging his leg again, clearing the space near Mother, making Howard have to dodge and back away.

No, Howard saw he'd been wrong: They didn't think he was just another goose—they thought he was a deranged, dangerous goose.

"Oh," the old witch told them airily, "some of the geese are wilder than the others." She swung her cane, moving faster than he'd have thought she could, and smacked him on the beak. "Go away," she told him. "Nobody here wants you."

"Mother, Father, Mother, Father, Mother, Father!" Howard honked frantically. Surely if he repeated it enough, they'd catch the human words beneath the goosely noise.

But they didn't.

"If you see him . . . ," Father said, raising his voice to be heard above the *him* they were searching for.

"Certainly," the witch assured them, the very picture of sympathetic concern. "If I see any sign of your poor missing little boy around here, I'll be sure to send word to you."

Howard stamped his webbed feet.

His mother looked frightened as she hurriedly told the old witch, "Thank you. You're very kind." Then she tugged on Father's sleeve, obviously anxious to get out of there. Her fear for Howard combined with her fear *of* Howard, and tears overflowed her eyes and ran down her cheeks.

"I . . . am . . . Howard," Howard honked so slowly and distinctly that they *had* to understand him.

Except they didn't.

They were leaving. His words were just honks to them, and they believed her, and they were leaving.

Howard flapped his wings, just enough to raise himself up to his parents' eye level.

"And she's not kind," he honked. "She's an old witch!"

His mother squealed, his father simultaneously shrank away and batted at him, and the old witch caught him in midair by grabbing hold of his neck.

He couldn't catch his breath and his webbed feet flapped helplessly out of reach of the ground. He was aware of his parents making a dash for the woods. With the little bit of air he had left, Howard used his best reasoning on the old witch: "Isn't it a good deed to try to keep a mother from worrying?"

"No," she hissed into his ear, "that's the least a child can do. Besides, you're not keeping her from worrying. You're frightening her and getting your father angry. Get it through your thick goose head: They don't know you."

She set him back down on the ground,

and Howard saw that his parents had already reached the forest in their hurry to get away from the mad goose they thought he was.

"Three," the old witch told him. "Good." She thumped her cane into the dirt for emphasis. "Deeds."

She stirred up enough dust that she started coughing, which gave Howard a certain amount of satisfaction.

But not much.

9

Old Friends

Three good deeds . . .

If his parents were not going to pay attention and be helpful, Howard would just have to do as the old witch wanted.

It can't be that hard, he reassured himself. He had stumbled into doing the first good deed almost right away. If the old witch was going to count such things as making a red-dyed goose feel better about herself, he expected he'd stumble into doing the second good deed at any moment now.

Any moment . . .

    Any moment . . .

        Any moment . . .

A week after Howard's parents had fled away from him—a week of goose conversation by day, a cold wet bottom by night, and coming to realize that the old witch's cast-off bread was indeed a treat—Roscoe came to Goose Pond.

Mighty-Beak/Bone-Crusher had just pecked Howard on the head for swimming too near to Sunset-Dances-Like-Flames-on-Her-Feathers—even though Howard hadn't even seen her.

Then Howard heard a familiar laugh.

It can't be, Howard told himself, not daring to believe his best friend had found him. Life was treating Howard too harshly lately, and he had begun to forget how to hope. But he swam out from the weeds he had been sulking in, just to see who it was who *sounded* so like Roscoe.

And there Roscoe was, dashing through the clear area between the forest and the edge of the pond, obviously intent on getting there without the old witch seeing.

Roscoe had come to rescue him.

Howard counted to six in the time it took before Roscoe dove into the safety of the tall weeds. Six was Howard's own best time from forest to weeds, and Roscoe was usually a step or two behind. Howard saw Roscoe stick his head up to make sure the old witch hadn't noticed him. But she didn't come storming out of the house to chase him off, which most likely meant she hadn't.

Howard raised his wings and was about

to honk a greeting, when Roscoe, facing
the forest, gestured for someone to come.

Alina stepped out from between the
trees.

Alina?

*Little Miss We-Haven't-Had-Goose-in-
Ages?*

And she was standing there like a block-
head, hesitating in plain sight, increasing
the probability that the old witch would
see her and chase both of them off.

No wonder Roscoe had covered the
distance so fast: He hadn't been concerned
with something as ordinary as evading the
old witch; he'd been trying to impress a
girl.

Roscoe once again waved Alina on,
and Alina ran for the high weeds.

Howard had time to count to nine.

Howard also had time to remember

how the villagers—starting with Alina's father—had thrown stones at him: step one
in the How-to-Cook-a-Goose recipe—
Dumphrey's Mill style. And how his own
parents had not recognized him even when
he had honked as clear as anything at them.
There was no way Roscoe could have
come to suspect Howard was here, trapped
in a goose body.

Roscoe wasn't here to rescue him after
all.

Maybe . . . , Howard insisted to himself,
trying to recapture that moment of relief
when he had first seen his friend.

*He can't know the old witch changed me into
a goose, but he COULD suspect she's done
something. So he'll be on the lookout for something unusual, some clue.*

Maybe Roscoe had brought Alina to
help him.

Somehow.

Just because Howard couldn't think of how Alina could be any help, that didn't mean Roscoe didn't have a plan.

But they seemed to be doing a lot of giggling for a rescue attempt.

Howard swam toward them, but slowly, keeping close to the weeds, watching from a distance.

"Look!" Alina squealed. But she wasn't pointing at him; she was pointing at the ground near the pond. "There's some!"

She was concentrating on her stomach again, on something goosey to eat, on eggs. Howard *knew,* because Roscoe and Alina had come out of the forest very near the spot he had come out a week and a half earlier, when he had found the nest and tried to make off with some eggs of his own.

He had stolen—and broken—three of the eight eggs from that nest; and he'd caused another to be lost when he'd rolled it toward the water to distract the goose mother and she hadn't been fast enough to prevent it from sinking into the water. (He had only learned that later, from goose gossip. Naturally, he'd never identified himself as having been formerly a boy, much less the sort of boy who would do such a thing.)

So there were four eggs left, which might be enough to satisfy Roscoe and Alina, with two each. Only now, Howard had come to know that particular goose. Her name was Can't-See-As-Well-Out-of-Her-Right-Eye-As-Her-Left, and fortunately she didn't recognize the goose How-Word as the boy who had cost her half her eggs. She was rather elderly, as geese went, and had just recently lost her longtime mate to a hunter's snare. She had been bemoaning that this, most likely her last clutch of eggs, would be so small.

Without a mate to take turns guarding the nest, Can't-See-As-Well-Out-of-Her-Right-Eye-As-Her-Left had momentarily left her nest to munch on some pond grass, but she saw the two humans and guessed what they had in mind.

"No!" Howard heard her honk. "Not my babies!"

No doubt Roscoe and Alina heard her honking, too, as she came skimming across the top of the water. The other geese all looked up at her frantic cries, but everyone could see she was too far away to get there in time to have any effect on the human children.

Howard, however, was not.

"Roscoe!" he honked, charging at his best friend and the girl he was with. He knew they couldn't understand him, but he was on a roll. "You big dolt! You lackwit! You numskull! If you aren't smart enough to rescue me, then you just get out of here!" He hissed, he flapped, he pecked.

Roscoe threw his arms up to protect his face. Alina screamed. Both backed away from the nest.

"I can't believe," Howard honked, "that you would forget me so soon! What are you doing, taking up with Alina, harassing innocent geese, laughing and having a good time, when you *should be LOOKING FOR ME!*"

Retreating backward, Roscoe tripped and fell. There was a stick, almost within range of his hand, and Roscoe tried to grab it, but Howard kept flapping his wings in his face.

The geese in the pond cheered.

Roscoe rolled over and used his hands to cover his head from attack.

Alina grabbed the stick and swung it at Howard, but she was afraid of getting hurt, and her movements were small and timid.

From the ground, Roscoe urged her, "Hit him! Hit him!"

How was *that* for a best friend?

Between Roscoe yelling and Alina still screaming, and a chorus of geese honking, "You get 'em, How-Word!" it took several moments before Howard became aware of another human voice, a voice that shouted: "Don't you *dare* hurt my geese!"

"Lady," Roscoe yelled back at the old witch, "who's attacking who?"

Howard stopped hissing and flapping. He was miserable enough being the only goose-shaped human on the pond; he could only imagine how miserable Alina and Roscoe would make him if the old witch transformed them, too, and they blamed him.

"Run, Roscoe! Run!" Alina cried, and she took off for the forest.

Roscoe scrambled to his feet, and he'd passed her before they reached the trees.

There goes my rescue, Howard thought.

But more than that, now that the excitement was over, he was remembering how much bigger humans are than geese. The realization washed over him that— if Roscoe had gotten to the stick or if Alina had been a better aim with it—the villagers of Dumphrey's Mill might have had goose dinner after all, compliments of Howard.

The thought would have made him break out into a cold sweat, if geese could sweat. As it was, he felt all tingly and light-headed.

"And don't come back!" the old witch yelled after the fleeing children. She shook her cane, though they were long gone.

She hobbled to the edge of the pond and leaned heavily on her cane. Her exertions had left her out of breath as she wheezed, "So that wasn't so bad, either."

Howard considered her words and evaluated the uncomfortable sensation he'd taken to be a combination of delayed fear and relief at having escaped injury. "You mean . . . ?" he asked.

Evidently the old witch wasn't interested in answering the obvious. Without a word, she made her way back to the cottage.

He had bravely faced danger to rescue Can't-See-As-Well-Out-of-Her-Right-Eye-As-Her-Left's unborn children—and apparently that counted as his second good deed.

The geese from the pond crowded

around him. "Yeah, How-Word!" they honked.

"Thank you, How-Word," said Can't-See-As-Well-Out-of-Her-Right-Eye-As-Her-Left.

"You're welcome," he said. Then, just in case the compliment-as-a-good-deed was working again, he added, "You're looking especially nice today."

"Thank you," she said again. But then she lowered her head and cocked it back as though ready to shoot forward, a gesture Howard had come to recognize as a goose's way of saying, *I don't think I like you*. She warned, "Now please step away from my eggs."

Howard did, and Mighty-Beak/Bone-Crusher bumped roughly into him, saying, "Not so close to my female."

Apparently some things changed, but others didn't.

10

Town Goose

Howard wasn't very quick with numbers, but he was quick enough to know that if you needed three good deeds, and you accomplished two good deeds, that left only one good deed to go.

Another set of numbers Howard was considering was that a week and a half had passed between Good Deed Number One and Good Deed Number Two. It had been a very long week and a half, and he was determined not to wait that long for

Good Deed Number Three to present itself. Surely, he thought, Roscoe would regain his courage or one of the other village
children would come to Goose Pond looking for eggs, looking for excitement, looking for something to do. Howard resolved
to scare that child off—rescuing a goose or
two, and being returned to his true size
and shape for his efforts.

Howard thought about this plan for a
day.

And another.

And a week.

What finally settled his mind that it was
time to do something rather than just wait
was when the old witch tossed some wilt-
ing, brown-edged lettuce leaves into the
pond, and the other geese practically
drowned him in their frenzy to gobble it
all up without leaving a scrap for him.

"Did you notice how I politely let

everybody else go first?" Howard called to the old witch. "Isn't being polite a good deed?"

Without even looking at him, the old witch gave a tired backhanded wave as she walked back to her cottage.

Howard didn't feel any of the bubbling sensation from what he thought of as the goose-turning-back-into-a-boy spell, so he gathered her answer was no.

All right, he thought. Apparently he had to go to Dumphrey's Mill to remind the children that there were geese at Goose Pond.

He hesitated. *What if . . . ?* he worried, letting his human boy mind flit with all the things that could go wrong while his goose body flew.

Better not to think, he thought. Then he threw himself into the air, while the other geese honked peevishly, demanding if something was wrong or if it was just that How-Word up to his taking-off-into-flight-without-warning trick again.

Irritated, Howard flapped his wings to get away from their squawking. Up, up, up into the air he went, and when he looked down he was amazed at how far up his wings had brought him. *I'm turning into a goose,* he thought. *My body is becoming used to being in this shape.*

That was not a comforting thought.

More than anything else, that assured him he was doing the right thing in not waiting. He needed to entice someone to come harass the geese so that he could heroically step forward again.

From up above, he saw the squares and rectangles of the fields.

He would have to be careful of the villagers—relatives and friends he had known all his life. He would have to make sure they saw him and got the idea of a goose dinner in their heads, without getting close enough to actually provide them with the opportunity for a goose dinner.

He flew low enough that he could see the people. It was, of course, spring, and spring was always a very busy time in Dumphrey's Mill, with walls and fences to be mended, fields to be readied for crops, roofs to be rethatched, newborn lambs and goats and pigs to be welcomed into the world. Even the children helped: older children alongside the adults, middle children looking out for the youngest, youngest on their best behavior while overworked parents' tempers were short.

If he were still a boy living at home, rather than a goose none of the other geese liked, Howard would have been helping, too.

Who could have ever guessed that

Howard would grow homesick for the opportunity to work?

Howard landed in the yard of the miller and gobbled up a few loose grains of barley that had spilled from someone's bag earlier in the day.

The miller and his son weren't grinding this afternoon. They were knee-deep in the stream whose current turned the big wheel that turned the stones that ground the grain. They were checking the wheel for pieces of wood that were warped or rotten and needed to be replaced. Howard figured this would slow them down when they came running out of the water to get him, so he could get away in time.

The son said to the miller, "There's that not-right-in-the-head goose again."

Not-right-in-the-head? First Alina's father called him *fat,* then the miller's son called him *not-right-in-the-head*?

"Something's wrong with that one," the miller agreed. "Any time a wild animal becomes too familiar, that's not a good sign."

Howard honked at him, but that didn't seem to change the fellow's mind.

The two men pulled loose old paddles from the wheel and hammered in new ones.

Howard kept alert for anyone sneaking up on him, but everyone around here looked too busy to pay him any attention at all.

After waiting awhile, he flew over to the house where Roscoe's family lived. There was no sign of Roscoe, but Gertrude was sitting on the stoop plucking a chicken. With the family's dinner already settled, this yard might well have been the safest place for him to be, but it was disconcerting to see all those feathers flying. Now that Howard was a goose, seeing that chicken plucked was almost like seeing a relative—a cousin or an in-law—dead and naked and destined for dinner.

Howard flew to the yard of another friend, Culbert—who was outside, seemingly in charge of his little brother and even littler sister.

The little girl saw him first and squealed, "Goose!" Unsteadily—but quickly—she ran forward, her arms held out as though she couldn't wait to get to him.

Howard would have let Culbert's sister get much closer, but Culbert yelled, "Stop!" and ran to catch up and sweep her into his arms. The girl tried to squirm loose, and Culbert scolded her saying, "The geese are mean this year."

"No," the girl insisted.

"Yes," Culbert said. "He'd bite you."

"Bite you," the little brother echoed in solemn warning.

"No," the girl said again.

"I think that's the mean one that chased Roscoe and Alina," Culbert said. Then, making a game of it, he said, "Don't let 'im get you!" and pretended to be the mean goose and chased his brother and sister around the yard.

Fat. Not-right-in-the-head. Mean.

How much worse could it get?

Howard saw his mother, carrying a basket of laundry that she was bringing back from the river.

Howard saw his mother see him.

Howard saw her tighten her hold on the laundry basket and cross the street to put more distance between them.

Howard drooped, from his head to his tail feathers.

It was time to go back to Goose Pond to try to come up with another plan.

II

Brave Goose

Howard began to look for an opportunity to show off his goodness by rescuing eggs or fledglings from someone besides a Dumphrey's Mill villager.

Did geese have anybody else to worry about? Howard wondered.

He didn't have to wonder long.

"Thief!" Howard heard the goose known as Scared-by-a-Rabbit shriek. "Thief! Thief! Get away from my nest!"

Scared-by-a-Rabbit was a highly nervous goose, and she generally honked for help at least once a day, so her frantic honking did not alarm the other geese. Her urgent cries had startled Howard several times during his first days at the pond, though he had never before been interested enough to investigate. Even Scared-by-a-Rabbit's mate, Always-First-to-Molt, could have moved faster to get to his female's side—except that he had had years of false alarms.

This time, however, Howard swam to the edge of the pond and waddled to her side as fast as his short goose legs could carry him. "What is it?" he demanded, turning his head this way and that to see where the danger was coming from. "What? What?" Then, to show how brave and thoughtful he was, he asked, "Is it more human children? Let me scare them away."

"Oh, never mind," said Scared-by-a-Rabbit. "It's just a clump of grass. For a moment there, I thought it was a badger." She pulled her head back, folding her neck on itself, the goosely first sign of wariness. "Just move away from my nest now, How-Word," she said. "My mate's on his way."

Howard got out of there before Always-First-to-Molt could hiss at him.

A badger, Howard thought. A badger was big. At least by goose standards. A badger had sharp claws and teeth. By anybody's standards. A badger could inflict a lot of damage.

Howard pictured himself as a boy trying to fend off a badger, and that seemed painful enough. He couldn't picture himself as a goose surviving such an encounter.

Howard had jumped into the middle of rescuing Can't-See-As-Well-Out-of-Her-Right-Eye-As-Her-Left's eggs from

Roscoe and Alina before stopping to think. Now he was relieved that Scared-by-a-Rabbit's danger had only been a menacing grass clump.

Maybe, he decided, he'd better be on the alert to find something else to take on: something a lot less dangerous than a badger, though probably a little more dangerous than a patch of grass.

More days passed.

Howard was waddling around on the grassy bank keeping alert for anything that looked risky-but-manageable when he noticed a white shape in the grass. It didn't look like a dangerous shape. In fact, it looked like . . .

"Egg!" he honked. "Someone's gone and lost an egg!" The egg was fairly near to the nest of a goose known as She-Who-Joined-Us-in-the-South and her mate, Almost-Eaten-by-a-Fox. The egg was near enough that She-Who-Joined-Us-in-the-South had just honked at Howard not to come any nearer.

She sat on her nest with her neck fully extended toward Howard, which might have been so she could get a better view of what he was looking at, or to warn him that she was suspicious of his intentions. Still, she sounded fairly untroubled as she asked, "What have you got there, How-Word?"

He pointed with the tip of his wing. "Egg," he repeated.

"Yes," she agreed without getting up.

Howard couldn't understand why she was taking this so calmly. He honked, "Someone lost one." He couldn't imagine how. Usually the geese were vigilant in their protectiveness of eggs. "We need to go around and have everyone count their clutches."

"Why?"

Howard wished he had hands with which he could shake her. "To find out where this egg came from."

"Oh," said She-Who-Joined-Us-in-the-South, "I can tell you that. It came from this nest."

I will never, Howard told himself, *understand geese.* He'd had a bump on his head two days ago from where Almost-Eaten-by-a-Fox had pecked him for wandering too close to the nest. He didn't say this. Instead he said, "Shall I roll it back to you?"

Did rolling count as saving?

Howard was fairly certain it should.

But She-Who-Joined-Us-in-the-South said, "No. I rolled it out myself. It's no good."

"No good?" Howard repeated.

"It will never hatch."

Howard rolled the egg over with his webbed foot. It looked like a perfectly fine egg to him. "How do you know it won't hatch?"

She-Who-Joined-Us-in-the-South had to stop and think. "It's not warm enough," she finally declared. "It doesn't move right."

Maybe there's a cold little goose in there, Howard thought, *who doesn't like to move much.* With none of her eggs hatched yet, it seemed too soon to assume that this one wasn't any good.

"You mean," he asked, "you don't want it?"

"No," She-Who-Joined-Us-in-the-South told him.

She-Who-Joined-Us-in-the-South was obviously more of an expert in eggs than Howard.

But still . . . , Howard thought. *It MIGHT hatch.*

Mightn't it?

Wouldn't it be a good deed if he rescued this egg from She-Who-Joined-Us-in-the-South's indifference?

"May I have it?" he asked.

She had begun to relax her neck, but now she once again pointed her beak straight at him, suspiciously. "Why?"

"To see if I can make it hatch."

She-Who-Joined-Us-in-the-South laughed. "You're a gander," she pointed out. "Ganders guard the females; females guard the eggs."

Other geese heard her honking and some started paddling this way, including Almost-Eaten-by-a-Fox.

"Does that mean you don't care?" Howard asked, eager to speed things up before he got pecked again.

Obviously anxious lest this be a trick,

She-Who-Joined-Us-in-the-South said, "You may have just that one."

Howard used his beak to roll the egg farther away from the nest. Almost-Eaten-by-a-Fox had gotten out of the water and now stood by his female, looking bigger and meaner than Howard.

"It's the won't-hatch one," Howard explained. "She said it was all right for me to have it."

Almost-Eaten-by-a-Fox continued to glower but didn't chase after Howard, so Howard resumed rolling the egg farther away.

Once the other two geese stopped watching him, Howard decided that must mean he had rolled the egg far enough.

Now what? He felt foolish about sitting on the egg, but that's what geese do. Howard was about to sit, when he remembered he needed a nest. The other nests were made with the females' down feathers, which he didn't have, and from leaves and grass, which he could gather.

He fetched enough to make a soft bed for the egg, then nudged the egg onto it. Then, very gently, he lowered himself on top.

A goose named Whistles-When-He-Honks called over to Howard, "Hey, How-Word, what are you doing?"

"Rescuing this egg," Howard said, since that was, after all, the long-range plan, and—he was sure—an admirable goal.

But Whistles-When-He-Honks laughed so hard he snorted pond water out his nostrils, and he called any other goose whose attention he could get to come and look at Howard.

They won't laugh when my good deeds get me turned back into a boy right in front of their eyes, Howard thought.

Then he thought, *I wonder how long it takes an egg to hatch?*

No matter. He could be patient.

If he had gotten hungry before, this was even worse, because he could no longer spend his days looking for plants to eat but instead had to keep the egg safe and warm.

Sitting on an egg was boring work— *long,* boring work, especially when all he could think about was how hungry he was. Every once in a while he just had to rush out to the water to graze on the plants at the edge.

One of those times, Sunset-Dances-Like-Flames-on-Her-Feathers swam to him. Howard looked up and saw Mighty-Beak/Bone-Crusher notice him and begin approaching. Before he could ask Sunset-Dances-Like-Flames-on-Her-Feathers to keep away lest her male beat him up anymore, she said, "There are tiny plants in the water, too, How-Word. Didn't they have those in the pond you came from?" She demonstrated by sticking her head into the muddy water, then chattering her beak to strain out the tiny bits of edibles.

Howard had seen the geese doing this before, but he had thought they were gargling. He knew enough not to say this.

Sunset-Dances-Like-Flames-on-Her-Feathers swam away before Howard could thank her, but also before Mighty-Beak/Bone-Crusher arrived.

Mighty-Beak/Bone-Crusher bobbed his head up and down to let Howard know that he wasn't getting away with anything, and Howard backed away.

But straining the water was a help, though the nourishment he got that way was even less tasty than the grasses and leaves.

Still, it was enough to keep him going for two days and two nights while he sat on the egg.

The third day, coming back from a few quick mouthfuls of tiny plants, water, and—of course—mud, Howard lowered himself onto his nest, and he felt something give.

Some instinct warned him this was not The Big Day.

He stood up. The egg had shattered, and there was no sign of a baby goose in there, just sticky, messy liquid.

Howard sighed.

All that time—wasted. Such a good plan—wasted.

And more than that: He realized he'd been picturing the tiny little goose that would come from the egg, a goose that wouldn't have existed, except for him.

But now it turned out there was no such thing.

He went to the water to wash the egg white off his feathers and to eat, and to forget the loss of the goose who never was. And to try to think up a new plan.

But of course he couldn't have wasted his efforts in private or had his failure go unnoticed.

"Say, How-Word!" one of the geese honked. "Hatched that egg of yours yet?"

Goose humor.

Howard hoped he wouldn't be a goose long enough to come to appreciate it.

12

Braver Goose

Howard continued to be on the look-out for good-deed-doing, and he happened to be in the vicinity when Scared-by-a-Rabbit once again honked for help.

Hoping it wasn't a badger, but growing desperate enough to think he might be persuaded to take on a badger (if it was a small one) Howard rushed to the anxious mother's side.

But it was neither badger nor clump of grass that had threatened her; it was a robin who had fluttered too close over her head. Even though robins never bothered geese, Scared-by-a-Rabbit explained to Howard that you could never tell: *This* might be the first robin that would turn vicious and would try to steal an egg.

"And why are you standing so close?" she demanded once she'd finished explaining. "Back away from the eggs."

Howard backed away.

Two days later, there was another attack at Goose Pond, but it wasn't reported by Scared-by-a-Rabbit, and this time Howard saw it all.

It was just coincidence that he happened to have glanced upward and noticed a black dot in the sky; and while he was still wondering what it was and why it was hurtling earthward, one of the other geese honked in terror, "Falcon!"

Moving faster than anything Howard

had ever seen before, the falcon swept out of the sky and grabbed a just-hatched fledgling from the nest of a pair whose names Howard didn't know. Then, with mighty beats of its wings, it angled upward before any of the geese could catch their breath. The parents honked in protest, bobbing their heads and hissing, but neither of them took to the air.

They're afraid, Howard thought.

Well, no wonder. A falcon was big. It was a meat eater, with a sharp beak and mighty talons that could puncture a poor goose's body.

But Howard was getting mightily tired of his own goose's body.

I will fly after that falcon, he thought, *and because I am so desperate to prove myself, I will be the fastest-flying goose there is, and I will catch up to him, and peck him until he lets that little fellow go, then I will catch that gosling midair. . . .*

But the first part of Howard's plan was *I will fly after that falcon,* and for some reason that didn't seem to be working.

Howard flapped his wings; Howard thought of himself as a goose, born to fly; Howard tried to throw himself up into the air.

Howard remained in the water.

Something was wrong with him.

The old witch! he thought. She wanted to keep him from doing that third good deed so that she wouldn't have to change him back into a boy.

"Help!" he honked. "Help!"

Some of the geese gathered around him. They could tell what was wrong with the family that had lost the gosling; they'd all seen goslings lost to predators before. But they couldn't tell what was wrong with him, so that was more interesting.

"What's the matter, How-Word?" they asked.

"It's not fair!" Howard slapped at the water with his wings. "The old witch has taken away my ability to fly, so I can't rescue any more of you."

The geese looked at one another. A soft noise started, which—for one brief moment—Howard thought was a murmur of sympathy.

It erupted into laughter. Hardly being able to keep a straight goose face, Sunset-Dances-Like-Flames-on-Her-Feathers said, "How-Word, you've molted."

Angry with her for not being more sympathetic, after he'd helped her—after even the old witch acknowledged that he'd done a good deed by helping her—he said, "Yeah? So I've lost some feathers."

"You've lost your flight feathers,"

Sunset-Dances-Like-Flames-on-Her-
Feathers explained.

"Because of the old witch?" Howard
asked in horror.

"Because of the time of year." She
flapped her wings.

Howard considered. He remembered
thinking that the goose parents were too
afraid to pursue the falcon, that he was
braver than they were. "You mean this
happens to all of you?" he asked.

The other geese were having a good
time with this. "That How-Word," they
honked. "Either he's the biggest joker in the
poultry kingdom, or he's as dumb as mud."

This was an especially stinging remark
since *he* thought *they* were slow-witted.

"What did you want to chase that falcon for, anyway?" Mighty-Beak/Bone-
Crusher asked. "That wasn't your gosling."

Howard's head drooped. "I wanted to do a good deed," he muttered at the water.

The geese spread away from him, chuckling to themselves. "That How-Word," they honked. "He's both a joker *and* dumb."

He didn't think he was either. But he was, still, a goose.

13

Bravest Goose

More days passed.

Some of those days the old witch came out to visit with the geese; some days she didn't.

What kind of caretaker was she? Howard thought peevishly. If he accomplished that third good deed, he wanted to make sure she was there to see it.

More of the eggs began to hatch— hatching order being a source of competition among the mothers and a matter of pride for the fathers. The fuzzy little goslings took to the water obviously born knowing how to swim. And how to call Howard "How-Word."

Then, one sticky afternoon, when it was too hot to move, Scared-by-a-Rabbit began screaming. "Thief!" she honked. "Thief! Thief! Thief!"

Howard hadn't seen another falcon, so he wondered if it was vicious-looking grass or another robin Scared-by-a-Rabbit thought was plotting to steal her eggs. Always-First-to-Molt slowly headed back to shore, and Howard—much closer—almost stayed where he was.

But, ever hopeful, he swam toward her. As he climbed up onto the bank, he came face-to-face with a rat—a rat with big long teeth and nimble fingers.

"Get away! Get away!" Scared-by-a-Rabbit shrieked, bobbing her head and flapping her wings at the fierce-eyed creature.

A threat. A real threat. Smaller than a badger, and unable to fly like a falcon.

Even knowing the rat could bite him, Howard lunged.

But instead of biting Howard, the rat bit the egg.

Howard tried to peck at the rat, but— either Howard wasn't as fast as Mighty-Beak/Bone-Crusher, who never had trouble connecting his beak with the top of Howard's head, or the rat was more skillful about dodging than Howard was. The rat clung to the egg, chewing away at the shell, gnawing, crunching, and sucking away at the inside.

Howard was able to peck the unrelenting creature once, a glancing blow. Still, it was finally enough to cause the rat to let go of the egg. But then it shifted its attention and teeth to Howard. It leaped, landing on Howard where his beak met his face. It bit. And it kept on biting. Holding on with its teeth, the rat dangled from Howard's face, kicking at Howard's throat with its sharp-clawed back feet.

Howard shook his head and flapped his wings, but the rat wouldn't come loose.

There's a rat on my nose! Howard screamed to himself. But he was too hurt and frightened to make any more sound than a hiss. Then he remembered: He was a goose. A goose who lived by a pond. Howard ran and stuck his head under the water.

Finally the rat let go.

Before Howard could decide if he was angry enough to go after the rat or frightened enough to never want to see it again, the rat paddled to the edge of the bank and disappeared into the weeds.

By then Always-First-to-Molt had made it to his mate's side.

"See?" Scared-by-a-Rabbit honked at him. "See? Didn't I say something was going to come after our eggs?"

Despite the throbbing in his face, Howard waddled up to them and winced at the remains of the egg, cracked wide open, with most—but not all—of the insides gone. "I tried to help," he said. He could feel the trickle of his own blood running down his beak. If he could only keep from fainting, surely the other geese would realize how brave he'd been.

"Go away, How-Word," Always-First-to-Molt ordered. "We have our other eggs to protect."

His tail drooping, Howard went to the old witch's cottage. He would have pecked at her door, but his beak was too sore for that, so he just honked until she came to investigate.

"Ooh," she said, "what's happened to you?"

"I fought off a rat," he told her. "Big rat." He held his stupid, flightless wings out to show how big.

The old witch was rummaging around through little pots and containers in her kitchen, which he would have thought meant she wasn't interested, but she asked, "After eggs, was he?"

"Yes," Howard said.

"Did he get one?"

Howard considered saying no, but he figured she would check with the other geese, making sure before she worked her magic on him. "Yes," he admitted.

The old witch found what she was looking for. "Come closer," she said.

Howard came forward, waiting to be changed back into a boy, though he wondered why, this time, she apparently needed some witchly potion.

She put something greasy on his beak. Something greasy that smelled like a bad combination of fir trees and fish. Something greasy and smelly—and that stung.

"Ouch!" Howard cried. "Is that supposed to turn me back into a boy?" He would be a greasy, smelly, sore boy with— he suspected by the feathers he was still losing—very little left of his clothing.

But he didn't turn back into his former shape, and the old witch said, "No, this is a salve to help you heal and to keep your nose from scarring."

"Well, that's very nice," Howard said, though—now that the excitement was over—he thought a little scar might make him look manly and bold. "But you mean you aren't going to turn me back into my real self?"

"Howard," she snapped at him. "Three. Good. Deeds. Not one. Not two. Three."

He supposed it was her way of saying that *trying* to save Scared-by-a-Rabbit's egg wasn't enough—even with injuries. "That's not fair!" he honked plaintively. "I tried. Trying should count."

"But what was your intent?" the old witch asked. "*Why* did you try?"

"To do a good deed!" Howard shouted at her.

"Yes, yes. That's my point." She shooed him out of the cottage. "Go away, I need to take a nap."

14

A Change
in the Wind

The days grew longer and warmer as spring bloomed into summer.

Those eggs that were going to hatch, hatched.

The goslings that came out of them grew from little balls of fuzz into geese just slightly smaller than their parents.

The adult geese, used to Howard or mellower now that there weren't young ones to protect, grew less territorial. Not friendlier, just less territorial.

And once in a while, with his belly full and the sun warm on his feathers, Howard would realize that a whole morning had passed, or a good part of an afternoon, without him worrying about his gooseliness—and that was the most worrisome thing of all.

What if, he asked himself, *I forget I'm a boy? What if I forget to keep looking for a chance to do something to break the spell?*

He could spend the rest of his life as a goose, and not even know anything was wrong.

Or, worse yet, he might—by purest coincidence—do a good deed then, and *then* the old witch would turn him back into a boy, just when he'd forgotten how to be one.

Scared by moments like these, Howard would get out of the water and sit on the bank, since that seemed more boylike than swimming aimlessly in the pond.

The goslings proclaimed him Not-Fun-How-Word and Stuck-up-Worse-Than-a-Swan-How-Word and had no more interest in him than their parents did—even Can't-See-As-Well-Out-of-Her-Right-Eye-As-Her-Left's youngsters, whom he'd saved from Roscoe and Alina.

One day one of the geese, Always-First-to-Molt, suddenly began to flap his wings. "Flight feathers are back!" he announced.

Other geese began to flap their wings. "Flight feathers," they honked, discovering their own. "Flight feathers!"

In a burst of joy, they took to the air, adults and younglings alike.

Caught up in the excitement, Howard joined them, before he realized what he was doing.

I am not a goose, he reminded himself. And he flew contrary to everyone else to settle back down on the grassy bank.

The old witch was in the yard, sitting on a stool, just enjoying the sunshine. "Not going to join the others?" she asked mildly. She shaded her eyes and murmured, "It's spectacular."

"I am a boy," Howard honked at her. "Boys do not fly."

"Your choice," the old witch said.

But it wasn't. Not really.

The days that had grown long now grew shorter, and sometimes the evenings were chilly. Sometimes the water was warmer than the air.

Certain flowers no longer bloomed.

The vegetation by the pond developed a distinctive taste—not better, not worse, just different—a taste Howard's goose sense labeled *autumnal*.

The leaves on the trees faded, not the light-but-bright green of first spring, but tired pale green, fraying into yellow—then almost overnight bursting into gold and orange and red.

And Howard was still a goose, with one more good deed to accomplish, and no idea what to do or how.

Now the pond was as chilly as the days almost always were—days of gusting winds that pulled the leaves from the trees, and dark clouds that threatened storms, which might be rain or might be something worse.

One afternoon, the old witch was tossing bread crumbs to the geese—which she had not been as good about doing as she'd been other years, or so the older geese had been complaining.

Some of them nibbled at the treat, but there wasn't the usual frenzy of gotta-get-some/gotta-get-some-*now*. Many of the geese were unsettled. Howard felt anxious, too, though he didn't know why—just restless and jittery. Many swam in tight circles, murmuring among themselves.

Passing by him, Can't-See-As-Well-Out-of-Her-Right-Eye-As-Her-Left asked, "Is it time?"

"Time for what?" Howard asked.

But she hadn't waited for an answer from him and was already headed toward some of the others. "Is it time?" she asked.

"Is it time?" they answered back.

Lackwit geese, Howard thought.

The murmuring grew louder.

Then shifted, from question to statement: "It is time. It is time."

"Time for what?" Howard demanded.

"It's time! It's time!" they honked back.

Howard could feel excitement building in him, even though he didn't know what was going on. The individual honks became synchronized into one single chorus as the geese honked together, so exhilarating that Howard joined in, whatever this was all about, until the feeling grew too large to be contained: "It's time! *It's time!* IT'S TIME!"

And then, all together—even Howard, though he'd had no idea what was about to pass his beak until it did—"Fly!"

The geese burst out of the water.

Once again—as on the day the geese had learned their flight feathers had grown back—Howard's enthusiasm dragged him along with them. *It can't hurt,* he told himself this time. *I'll fly a little bit.*

The geese wheeled back and forth, swooping up, then down, turning one way then the other.

Howard was having a good time despite himself.

Far below the old witch was waving. "Good-bye!" she called. "Good-bye. Have a safe journey. Good-bye, Red-Beak. Good-bye, Limp-Tail. Good-bye, He-Who-Honks-the-Loudest."

Journey? Howard thought as the old witch called off names.

As the old witch called off names?

That was something he remembered from the folklore of Dumphrey's Mill, part of the old witch's craziness: She would tend the geese in the spring, and then stand in her yard yelling good-byes when they flew south for the winter.

South: the direction the flock—after its veering and dipping—had finally started off in.

"Wait!" Howard practically stopped in

midair, and another goose almost collided with him. "We're *leaving*?"

"Watch where you're flying," that one muttered as he swerved to avoid Howard.

"Watch where you're flying. Watch where you're flying," others complained as those who had been behind began to catch up and bypass him.

"We're leaving?" Howard repeated. He couldn't leave. Dumphrey's Mill was here. His parents were here.

The witch who could change him back into his real shape was here.

Howard flapped just enough to keep up with the stragglers. "You're heading south?" he asked. "For the winter?"

"Oh, How-Word!" one of the geese called over his shoulder—Howard wasn't sure, from this back angle, who—"You always say the funniest things!"

Of course they were heading south for the winter. That's what geese do.

Howard slowed even more.

If I go with them, he thought, *and I do a good deed, how will the old witch know and be able to turn me back into a boy?*

But if I stay here, without them, who will I be able to do a good deed for?

He had already tried complimenting the old witch herself, and that hadn't had any effect. And he couldn't see how he could ever rescue her from anyone or anything. Someone with magic simply wasn't dependent on a goose, no matter how brave.

In Dumphrey's Mill, he couldn't compliment anyone, because no one there spoke goose. And if he stayed around the village, on the lookout to rescue them from something or other—who knew what?—they were sure to eventually catch him and throw him into a cook pot.

Was that supposed to be his third good deed? he wondered crankily: To feed a hungry family?

Someone had angled away from the others and was coming back for him: the goose still known as Sunset-Dances-Like-Flames-on-Her-Feathers, though the red dye was just about all gone. "How-Word," she honked. "Catch up."

"I can't go south with the flock," he said. Perhaps she would be a loyal friend and offer to stay with him.

Instead she said, "Oh. All right then. Good-bye, How-Word." She swung around again and rejoined the formation.

Howard stayed in the air, flying back and forth across the pond, as the sound of their honking faded.

Until all the geese were so far away their individual shapes merged into one single shape.

Which became smaller and smaller.

And then was gone.

Alone, he flew down to the yard of the old witch.

She had been heading back to her cottage, but now stopped to lean on her cane and ask, "Decided to stay?"

Howard cocked his head to get a better look at her, to try to read her expression. "*Should* I have gone?" he asked. Fine time to ask, now that it was too late.

The old witch shrugged. "It's going to get cold here," she said.

Which sounded like a yes to Howard.

Frantically, he demanded, "Should I try to catch up? Should I try to find them? If I do a good deed while I'm in the south with them, will you know it and turn me back?" That was a sudden bad thought. "Would you turn me back while I'm in the south with them, so that I'd have to get back here on my own, walking?" Howard wondered how far south *south* was. "Or would you wait until we came back next spring?" Waiting wasn't good, either. Why was he even asking? He knew he could never catch up now. "Why didn't you tell me before that I should go with them?"

"Howard," the old witch said, "you're making me tired. Leave me alone." She sat down on the stoop by her door as though she didn't even have the energy to get away from him indoors.

"*You're* tired?" Howard said. "Try being a goose for a while, and see how tired that makes you." He started to waddle toward the pond then decided he'd better check whether she planned to feed him, now that he was stuck here for the winter. "Speaking of cold . . . ," he began.

She hadn't moved, except for dropping her cane.

But Howard knew she hadn't fallen asleep.

The old witch had died.

15

Howard and the Old Witch

Howard sat down heavily in the dust by the old witch's feet.

Now he would never regain his boy's body.

He was stuck as a goose as surely as those born to it.

What were his choices? He could spend the winter here, alone, hoping a solitary goose—a goose without much experience as a goose—could survive the harshness of the weather and the scarcity of food. Or he could start flying southward and hope to catch up to the Goose Pond geese when they stopped for the night. That was assuming he could find them, of course. Or he might happen upon another flock of geese—and he could start all over with them. If they let him.

Whichever he chose, he would never have a chance to explain to his parents what had happened. They would die never knowing whether he'd run off or been killed. Actually, now that he thought about it, he would probably die first. Under the best of circumstances, geese don't live as long as people, and his were certainly not the best of circumstances.

He looked at the dead old witch, with her head leaned back against the door, her gray wispy hair lifting in the wind.

Your fault, he thought.

But he couldn't hate her.

She had been ailing, slowing down, all spring and summer long. She had not gone into Dumphrey's Mill once during that time, and the only ones who had come here had been his parents, looking for him, and Roscoe and Alina, looking for eggs. No one had cared enough to worry about her, and that had to be hard, whether you were a witch or not.

She was still ugly, she was still old, she was still mean—but Howard couldn't just leave her like this, sitting dead on the stoop.

He flew up to the window and into the cottage. The room was messier, dustier than it had been the time she had let him in to tend his rat-bitten beak. He saw no store of wood set by the fireplace in preparation for the winter cold, the way his family would have done by now. And there didn't appear to be much food left: The bread she had been throwing out to the geese looked to be close to the last of what she had.

In the corner was her bed, and there he saw what he needed. He waddled over, then tugged with his beak at the corner of the blanket. It came loose, and he managed to drag it off the bed and across the floor.

But then he realized that the old witch was sitting on the other side of the door, so he'd never be able to push it open.

He took as much of the hem of the blanket in his beak as he could manage, determined to fly out the window. But the weight of the blanket hanging loose was too much, and the blanket slithered back down to the floor.

Howard poked and prodded with beak and webbed feet, until finally he managed to fold the blanket, more or less halfway lengthwise, then again widthwise.

This made the blanket rather thick for beak holding, and he dropped it twice more before, on his third attempt, he got most of it onto the windowsill.

Then, from outside, he tugged it down onto the ground.

Something that would have been so easy for a boy half his age had taken him the greater part of the morning to accomplish as a goose.

Stupid, he called himself.

Waste of a good blanket that could keep ME warm come this winter, he told himself.

But he knew he couldn't really survive the winter on his own, with or without a blanket.

So he dragged it to the feet of the old witch, and then—with just as much difficulty as he'd had folding the thing in the first place—now he managed to unfold it. Lastly, he pulled it up over her, covering her the best he could, because that, he knew from when his grandmother had died, was what decent people did, as though the dead person would not want people gawking.

Not that there was anybody around to gawk at the old witch.

Now what?

Blanket or not, animals would come.

That can't be helped, Howard thought. *If she'd turned me into a dog, then—MAYBE— I could have buried her.*

It was her own fault.

But if he couldn't bury her, maybe he could find someone who could. If he went to Dumphrey's Mill, and if he pretended to have a broken wing, he might entice someone to chase after him in hope of an easy meal, someone he could lead back here, someone who would see the dead old witch and do the right thing.

It was a dangerous plan. If Howard was to convince people he couldn't fly, then—obviously—*he couldn't fly*. And they might catch him, during that long trek through the woods. They might catch him and wring his neck before he could escape.

He wondered if, dead, his body would resume its true shape.

That would be an unpleasant shock for someone.

Someone who deserved it, if they'd wrung his neck.

Howard knew going back to Dumphrey's Mill might be the last thing he would ever do. But as his future looked so bleak anyway, he decided to chance it.

Still, he felt—since he might not make it back—that he should say a few solemn words over the old witch. Not that honking generally came out sounding solemn. But that was what the villagers had done for his grandmother: called back pleasant memories, shared nice things about her.

Howard hadn't really known the old witch well enough to be able to think of much he could say about her, and what he knew for the most part didn't seem appropriate: *She loved geese but hated people?*

He thought again of how no one had come looking for her in all these months.

She was good at ruining the lives of innocent boys by turning them into geese?

Well, not *that* innocent: She'd caught him stealing the eggs of the geese who were her only friends—frivolous and silly as those geese were.

She put salve on my nose when I got bitten by a rat?

Howard stepped forward with the only thing he could think of. He said, "I'm sorry I was mean to you, and I forgive you for being mean back to me."

No sooner had the honks passed his beak than his feathers began to vibrate, his skin began to bubble, his bones made a screeching noise like nails being pulled out of wood.

Howard tipped over, and when his eyes uncrossed as he was sitting there in the dirt, he saw long, thick legs ending in sensible, unwebbed feet; he saw arms instead of wings; he saw cloth and skin rather than feathers: He was a boy again—proof that the witch's spell worked by itself, without needing her to be aware of what he'd done.

Howard looked at his hands, and thought his fingers were the most marvelous things he had ever seen. He threw his head back and yelled—yelled, not honked—"Hurray!" He liked the sound of that so well, he jumped up and—a bit unsteadily on his new old feet—ran a circle around the outside of the cottage, yelling, "Hurray! Hurray! Hurray!"

Once he stopped for a breath, he noticed that he was, indeed, still wearing clothes. They even looked—for the most part—like what he'd been wearing that day in early spring, except that certain patches seemed brighter or thicker or, well, *newer* than the rest.

The sight of the blanket-covered body of the old witch returned a sense of seriousness to him. He was sure she must have a shovel since she had a vegetable garden, but burying her no longer seemed the right thing to do.

He tied the blanket more securely around her shoulders, then set about moving her. Being so old, she had shrunk down to a size close to Howard's own and she didn't weigh very much, which meant he was able to get her to the edge of the pond, and then into the water where she could be, come spring, among the geese.

"I hope that's what you wanted," he said, and only then did he set off for home.